Cosy

VALKYRIE ACADEMY DRAGON ALLIANCE
Book One

CHOSEN

"Asgard has two kinds of Valkyries, winged and wingless. The wingless Valkyries are treated like slaves, but headstrong teenager Kara is determined to change that, and with the help of a powerful dragon, she just might get her chance."
Susie D., Line Editor, Red Adept Editing

VALKYRIE ACADEMY DRAGON ALLIANCE BOOKS

.

Cosy Burrow Books

VALKYRIE ACADEMY DRAGON ALLIANCE

CHOSEN

KATRINA COPE

Dusk ~ For your endless love and dedication **;)**

GET UPDATES & NOTIFICATIONS OF GIVEAWAYS

Would you like a FREE copy of Marked?
Visit here:

https://www.katrinacopebooks.com/valkyrie-academy-dragon-alliance

Through this link you can sign up for my newsletter and receive a FREE copy of Marked plus updates about my fantasy books, sales and notification of giveaways.

- CHAPTER ONE -

A horn blares, and I run outside the academy walls to watch the ascension of the winged Valkyries to the rainbow bridge. There could only be one explanation for the horn–a war in Midgard, and warriors are falling. The winged Valkyries flock to Heimdall's post, the entrance of Bifrost, seeking departure from Asgard and entrance into Midgard. Envy stirs deep within when I think about their mission–to find the brave warriors of either side and reap their souls to send to Valhalla in preparation for

Ragnarok. It is a mission that is denied to me and my kind. Awe envelops me as I watch them take flight with their beautiful majestic wings flapping and raising them high.

A piercing alarm bell rings throughout the school, and a sense of urgency flutters through my body. I pull my eyes away and rush past Asgard's harsh landscape to the center hall, where we're expected to gather every time the alarm sounds. This is my third year at Valkyrie Academy, leaving one year to go. After receiving a formal education, the Valkyries are sent to the academy from ages fifteen to eighteen to finish their training for their duties, which they will undertake for the rest of their immortal lives.

"Wait up, Kara. What do you think they need us for?" Eir moves in beside me. She pulls a hairband off her wrist and ties back her long light-brown hair, securing her wavy locks neatly out of her face. Her kind face creases, and her light-brown eyes fill with worry.

"Perhaps for once, they are giving us something important to do." Hildr joins me on my other side, clasping the hilt of her sword, looking ready for action, even though we're not going to war.

"I doubt it," I say, and her green eyes focus on me with such annoyance that I think I see her short spiky red hair stand on end. "Hey, don't kill the messenger." I hold my hands up in defense. "You know where I stand with the bias against our wingless kind."

She huffs as we enter the academy hall. We scurry to find a seat around the outskirts, watching our mistress stand in the middle.

The winged Valkyries file in and sit in the reserved seats in the rows closer to the mistress. On one hand, I loathe that they are treated like royalty among the Valkyrie, but on the other, I long to be part of what they can do.

My eyes narrow as my nemesis enters the room, flanked by her two accomplices, Mist and Prima. They look as though they were made from the same molding cast. Rota's perfect waves of blond hair fall to her shoulders, and her slim figure in her tan leather jacket and tight blue pants is framed by her beautiful, majestic white wings. She is beautiful in every way, as a Valkyrie should be. I don't

3

despise her for this. Even the wingless Valkyries are known for being beautiful. My distaste for her is based more on how she treats my kind, me in particular. It isn't unusual for the winged Valkyries to pick on the wingless ones, as we are seen as lower class, but this particular one has taken it to another level with me. For some reason, she has taken an interest in tormenting me in my daily life in the academy right from my very first day. Perhaps it is because she knows that I've strived to be one of the winged Valkyries and how I long for the myth of how Brynhildr got her wings to come true.

Rota is holding her head high with an air of superiority as the three take the prime seats, directly in front of the mistress. Deep-green envy runs through my veins. I wish that, for once in my life, I could wipe the smug looks off their faces.

As everyone scrambles into the room, the ruckus of the hall is overbearing. The mistress raises her hands. "Now, Valkyries, students, quiet down." When the hall remains noisy, she raises her voice some more. "You must be silent this instant. We have an urgent matter to discuss." The noise in the hall remains the same. Her voice crescendos. "Valkyries! Be quiet now!"

The hall falls silent. It is surprising that the hall remained as loud as it did for so long. We all know that if we do not listen to the mistress, the punishment is severe. Shuffling shoes echo through the hall as some straggling Valkyries hurry to their seats.

A flicker of annoyance passes over Mistress Sigrun's face before being washed away by control. "There is a war on Midgard, and we do not have enough Valkyries to reap the brave warriors. As you know, we need these courageous warriors to train here so that they will be ready to defend Asgard when the day of Ragnarok arrives." Her eyes land on the winged Valkyries, and a sense of pride fills her face. "My top students, it is now your time to undergo your first reaping."

A murmur echoes through the hall, and the mistress raises her hands again, causing the hall to fall silent. "We knew this time was coming, and for the senior students, your opportunity is now. You have trained hard and trained well."

Without meaning to, I look at my nemesis, and I can't help glowering. Her face is overflowing with pride and arrogance in knowing that she's about to have her first reaping. She knows that soon, her name will be honored among the Valkyries and spoken of in the halls of Valhalla. I don't think it is possible for me to loathe her any more than I do right at this moment.

The mistress raises her arms again, calling for attention. "Valkyries, let us leave and head to Heimdall's point. Time is of the utmost importance."

A rustling of feathers echoes through the room as the winged Valkyries stand and exit the hall, leaving the wingless Valkyries in their spots, and a potent disappointment tarnishes the atmosphere. Because we are not winged, we are not permitted to go to these battles.

Pausing at the entrance of the hall, the mistress spins around to add insult to injury. "Oh, and don't forget to clean the hall of Valhalla. I'm sure the claimed warriors had a large party last night and have left it a mess after drinking too much mead. The hall must be cleaned and ready for the new group of warriors so that they may be impressed by our hospitality."

Although she's the mistress, I can't help but glare at her with all the hostility I can muster. I want to prove my worth, and I am sure we have special gifts as well. My sword's sheath rubs against my black leather pants as though reminding me it is there.

Without another word, the mistress spins around and follows her prize possessions up to the bridge in a sea of tan leather jackets and blue leather pants—their Valkyrie uniform.

"I want to punch someone!" Hildr's feet are planted firmly on the ground with her knees shoulder width apart. She sits forward, and her black leather pants squeak as her elbows twist into them.

Eir reaches over me and places her hand on Hildr's back. "Chill. There is more to life than fighting."

Hildr's voice explodes with aggression. "Just because you're willing to go with the flow doesn't mean I can't be angry about our role. Are they ever going to let us fight with them? Kara and I are incredible fighters. Even you are, too, when you put aside your peacekeeping intentions."

I rise and head for the door.

"Where are you going?" The anger in Hildr's voice remains, but I ignore it. I know it is aimed toward the winged Valkyries and their rules.

I turn around to look at her. "I'll meet you in the hall soon. I'm going to watch them ascend."

Hildr huffs. "Do you think I need any more salt rubbed into my wound? There is no way I am going to watch them ascend into glory."

Eir gives me an understanding smile. "Don't do anything stupid. They would love to give you more menial jobs, I'm sure, if they catch you at Heimdall's point instead of cleaning the hall."

Turning, I cast her a smirk over my shoulder. "I'll be stealthy." I quicken my pace and stop at the weapons wall outside of the hall, grabbing a bow and throwing a quiver full of arrows over my back before heading straight to Heimdall's.

The sky lights up with a rainbow of colors then dulls again as Bifrost straightens. The first lot of Valkyries is released into Midgard. A few moments later, another large flash goes through the rainbow colors filling the sky, and I know that the next lot of Valkyries has gone — the Valkyries from the academy. It is only seconds before Bifrost straightens, lining the sky in a nice neat rainbow.

I head in that direction. Maybe I can find a way to sneak past Heimdall and help the winged Valkyries reap the souls with or without their approval.

- CHAPTER TWO -

By the time I reach Bifrost, my legs ache. It's far away from the academy, and the journey ends with an extensive climb, a feat that the winged Valkyries don't have to accomplish. They land with ease, using the power of their wings, an option not available to me. Instead, I had to climb the rocky terrain, ascending to the point of the tower.

Placing my hands on my hips, I catch my breath and study the rainbow bridge stretching far and wide. I observe the straight lines and follow them all the way until they reach the small tower where Heimdall stands with his legs in a ready stance. His towering bulk is covered in armor, a horned helmet protects his head, and his hands are planted over the hilt of his sword while he guards the entrance to the other worlds, scanning with his all-seeing eyes. I'm sure he is also watching the Valkyries' progress into Midgard.

Ignoring my exhaustion and the pain surging through my legs, I approach Heimdall. His eyes slowly turn, and he gazes at me as the distance between us closes.

"Young Valkyrie of the wingless kind. You have traveled far. What is your purpose?" His eyes bore deep into my soul, as though he's reading my intentions. From what I have heard, he is not able to read our thoughts, but he does know what we do.

I square my shoulders and step forward with confidence that I don't feel, doing my best to steady my breath. "Heimdall, I wish to join the winged Valkyries and help them reap the brave warriors for Valhalla."

The corners of his eyes twitch up, and his

eyes dance for a moment, as though he is about to break into a smile. He quickly pushes his mouth into a flat line. "Young Valkyrie, you are courageous, but this is not your destiny. You must turn around and go back."

"But I believe I can help." The words come out faster than I intend, sounding urgent, almost desperate.

"Your intentions are good, young Valkyrie. But this is not permitted. It is the Asgard way. You must return to your academy. I will inform your mistress that you are willing to drop everything to help the cause."

My mistress's likely response flickers through my mind, and my heart sinks. Her face would break into a smile, and she would laugh despite my wanting to help and my intentions being good. I know if anything, it will just be a joke to her.

"No, don't bother. This can remain our secret." I let my eyes trail to the tower, the entrance of which I can use to leave this realm and go into Midgard. And my heart longs to enter there. I can feel his eyes studying me, taking in everything that he is seeing, and I'm sure it is an unforgettable memory that he will store away. I so badly want to go and help. Surely I can be of more use than cleaning the halls and being almost a slave to the winged Valkyries.

As I stare at the entrance, a voice enters the depths of my mind, deep and rumbling. *Go, young Valkyrie. Despite what he says, it is your destiny. You are more important than what they make you believe.*

I look at Heimdall to see if he's the one talking in my mind. Perhaps it is a gift he holds that I don't know about. I search the depths of his dark-brown eyes, which peer out from under the canopy of his large horned helmet, and see no sign lying in them that it is him. Maybe this is a joke he plays when faced with someone opposing the rules of Asgard's borders. He is the watchman of the gods and the gatekeeper to Bifrost. *If he is not the one that is telling me this, then who can it be?* I cast a brief look around but cannot see anyone else.

A deep, searing pain shoots from my shoulder and down my right arm. I flinch and clutch at it, grimacing.

"Young Valkyrie, what is wrong?" Heimdall moves forward, concern in his eyes.

I yank back my black leather sleeve, revealing my shoulder, and peer down at the initiating point of the pain. The scar that I received a couple of years ago has turned bright red and is burning. I place a hand over it, protecting it, as though that'll help the pain go away, but it does not feel any better, so I rub it, trying to work away the pain.

Heimdall's eyes are wide. "Where did you receive this mark, young Valkyrie?"

After seeing no new damage, I cover my shoulder. "Some beast attacked me one day when I was in the dragon fields. I had stumbled across a nest of dragon eggs. It was trying to steal them, and I went to stop it. I managed to scare the beast away from the dragon eggs, but it clawed me as it took off, leaving me with this scar." I rub the spot harder through my clothes. "It has never burned like this before."

"What kind of beast?"

At first, I am shocked by his question, until it occurs to me that he wouldn't know, as he doesn't watch what happens in Asgard all the time. Instead, his eyes are focused on outside threats.

"I don't know."

His brow furrows, and something flits over his shoulder. It takes an effort to peer around his bulky form, and my eyes widen as they land on the same beast that caused the mark on my shoulder. I hadn't seen it since the day it injured me.

"It was *that* beast," I say, pointing past Heimdall.

He spins and lifts his sword a split second before the beast lunges for him, managing to block the beast's attack. The beast lunges at him again then maneuvers back before the mighty protector of Asgard can strike.

Even though my shoulder is throbbing, I am still determined to make my way to Midgard to see if I can help the winged Valkyries. The thought of helping the great gatekeeper fight off the beast passes through my mind, but as I watch him, I am confident that he will be able to defeat it. He is an extremely large warrior.

While Heimdall is distracted, I run to the

tower, the entrance to the portal. Behind me, I can hear the beast continuing to attack the great guard of Bifrost, yet neither seems to be successful in striking the other. No cries of pain come from either one.

I reach the portal entrance and hold the knob with both hands. When I turn to see Heimdall, the beast is moving in for another attack. He spins and swipes his sword at it but misses as the beast flaps its wings and darts away. The creature's beady eyes land on me, and a piercing squawk fills the air before it flaps away.

Heimdall's distraction is disappearing into the distance, and I am about to miss my opportunity. I brace myself, ready to turn the key, when Heimdall spins and spots me at the portal.

"No, young Valkyrie!" His large form takes enormous steps as he runs toward me, closing the gap between us quickly.

I have to act now. With my heart thumping quickly, I twist the knob. Heimdall is only seconds away from me as a bright, colorful light surrounds me, and I feel myself being sucked into a vacuum as though I am on a slippery slide twirling downward. Dizziness engulfs me, so I close my eyes, knowing I can do nothing other than go with the flow until I land with a thump.

My butt aches from the rough landing. I place my hands on either side of me and feel a solid surface with something rough tickling my palms, then I open my eyes and blink a couple of times before gazing down to see green strands protruding out of the hard, grey dirt. It is some kind of foliage that softens the hard earth, and I notice that it covers nearly every part of the ground. Midgard almost looks green. It is beautiful.

I gaze into the distance to see large brown trunks reaching for the sky, and branching out of them are limbs covered with green foliage framed by a crystal-clear blue sky. These must be what they call trees. And from what I see, they are more beautiful than how they were described.

A soft rustling surrounds me as the wind whips my black hair away from my face. I breathe in deeply, taking in the fresh air. It smells beautiful, almost sweet, unless that is the pale-pink flowers I spot not too far away. Instantly, I know I am in love with Midgard. But a scream that pierces the air stops my daydreaming.

- CHAPTER THREE -

I spring to my feet, spin around, and run up the hill. As I reach the crest, I am devastated by the scene playing out before me. Massive amounts of men and women are fighting each other, and brave warriors are dying in all directions. I watch as the winged Valkyries fly above them and land in certain spots, fighting off the angels of death before reaping the bravest warriors that they can find. The soldiers that they reap will be another mark of honor against their name in aid to Valhalla and a proud contribution to the mighty warriors that will fight in Ragnarok. A twinge of envy pierces my heart as I watch them undertake this honor with their graceful wings.

A rumble rolls across the sky, and I think that perhaps Heimdall is searching for someone to come and retrieve me. I spring into action. I'm not going to miss out on this. It's my chance to prove that the wingless Valkyries are worth more than what the winged Valkyries give them credit for. We have trained to fight and are spectacular warriors on the ground.

The soldiers push forward toward a massive wall, stepping over their fallen comrades, and the Valkyries gracefully swoop down one by one and land next to the fallen and reap their souls. The ones that they do not reap are left for the angels of death.

A group of soldiers hunkers down and aims a cannon at the wall, lights it, fires, and watches the explosion destroy the ramparts. Even from this distance, screams rumble across the plain. A Valkyrie swoops down to the wall to claim the souls of the brave soldiers before they pass away. As she lands, a dark-winged male swoops down and lands next to her. I've learned about them at the academy. These winged beings are the angels of death—the largest threat to our victory.

The Valkyrie unsheathes her sword and starts to fend off the angel of death, who is eager to grab these soldiers and take them back to the underworld. She slices at him, and he dodges with nimble feet, narrowly missing her blade. A dark shadow passes over the corner of my eye, and I turn to see another angel of death hovering over a wounded soldier that has not been spotted by a Valkyrie.

I pull an arrow from my quiver and nock it then draw it back and aim the tip at the angel of death. "Stand back. This one's mine," I call across the distance.

The angel of death halts. His black eyes peer through his strands of dark hair that have fallen over them. These angels have been our lifelong enemies, and we need to defend our future soldiers against them so we can train the soldiers to fight in the final war of Ragnarok. But as he peers at me, I am taken aback by how young his skin looks and how striking the lines are in his chiseled jaw. He flicks his head, and the hair moves out of his eyes. I think I see amusement in them.

He stands planted on the spot. His black leather pants cling to his legs, and a fitted black T-shirt hugs his chest, defining the muscles of his torso. My teachers told me a lot about the angels of death, but they never discussed how attractive they were. This is the first one I've seen face-to-face.

Trying to wipe the sight of his body out of my mind, I focus on his eyes, but he is rather distracting, and an amused smile gleams from his eyes.

"What do we have here?" His voice is so deep and smooth that it almost sounds like he is singing his words.

Slowly, I move toward him with my arrow remaining pointed at him. He keeps his hands raised, watching me as I continue forward, ignoring his question and taking my time assessing the situation.

"What are you?" he asks. He peers over my shoulders as though looking for something. "You're not a Valkyrie. That's for sure."

Anger heats my face, but I bite my tongue. As much as I want to shoot my mouth off at him, I don't want to give him any information he doesn't already have.

"What's wrong? Did I say something wrong?"

My heart catches in my throat. I never thought a voice could sound so beautiful yet taunting at the same time. Within a few moments, he has found a way to get under my skin.

After weighing up my choices, I answer him without bothering to hide the spite in my voice. "I'm a Valkyrie. And if you don't shut up, I'll shoot this arrow through your arm."

His smirk grows wider. "A Valkyrie? But you don't have any wings."

My eyes shoot daggers at him, and I shake the arrow slightly, pulling his attention back to it. "Remember, your arm?" I aim the arrow directly at his arm again.

"I was merely saying." He shrugs. "No need to get so irritated over it. I've never seen the likes of you before. Every Valkyrie has wings."

"No. Not every Valkyrie has wings. A large

amount of us don't." *So much for withholding information.*

"Well, in that case, my name is Harut. It is nice to meet you." His smile broadens. "Your name was?"

"I didn't say."

"No, you didn't. But I was trying to make friends. We don't have to be enemies, you know."

Movement catches my eye, and I see a Valkyrie fighting off an angel of death over the potential warrior. I glance back at him. "Yeah, it really looks like we can be friends," I say with sarcasm.

"Why can't we be friends? You're the first Valkyrie I've seen without wings. Where do they keep you if there are so many of you?" His intentions seem innocent enough, yet I can feel the rush of blood to my face again.

"That good, is it?" He cocks his head. "I guess they don't treat you well, looking at your reaction."

"They treat us like second-class citizens," I snap.

"So how did you end up here?"

"I snuck past Heimdall and traveled Bifrost when he was distracted by some creature."

"That's daring." He raises an eyebrow.

"I'm dying to prove that we are worth just as much as the winged Valkyries. I want to reap a soul for Valhalla–to prove the point. We train as warriors just as much as they do, but they never let us on a battlefield because we lack wings."

He indicates the soldier, who is still groaning on the ground, only moments away from dying. "In that case, be my guest."

I look at the soldier then back at the angel of death. "Really?"

He nods.

"Thank you." I'm about to squat when a guilty rush hits me. He's been kind to me, and I haven't even told him my name. "I'm Kara."

He smiles broadly again, showing many straight white teeth. "Nice to meet you."

I feel a different kind of redness flowing to my face. Quickly, I dart my eyes down to the warrior dying on the ground and squat before him.

I haven't done this before, although I believe that when we touch humans, this is what happens. My heart thumps rapidly as I reach down to touch the soldier's skin. I hope this works. So much is riding on it.

- CHAPTER FOUR -

Bracing myself, I take a deep breath. This is breaking new territory for me and all the wingless Valkyries. After composing myself, I place my hand on his skin.

"What are you doing?" A voice booms over my shoulder.

I balk and turn to find Rota standing beside me. Her hands are on her hips, and she stands with her feet firmly planted. "You shouldn't be here. What in Vigrid do you think you are doing?" Her gaze travels from my hands to the wounded soldier. "You should be back in Asgard, cleaning the Valhalla hall and getting it ready for us to celebrate, not standing here wasting time. They're our soldiers to reap, not yours. You will never be a reaper."

Harut opens his arms. "Give her a chance. Everyone must be able to prove themselves at some point. Why should she go back and clean the halls?"

"Stay out of this, angel of death. This is none of your business."

He takes a step toward her, and she pulls her sword from its sheath. The sound of sliding metal rings through the air. A breeze passes from the angel of death's direction, and a putrid smell fills my nose. I breathe it out and try to search past him over the grassy plain, right up to the edge of the trees. It smells like bodies decaying. I frown. This war field is too new for any bodies to be decaying. A dead animal that I cannot see must be lying in that direction.

A high-pitched whistle screams, and my shoulders slump. Rota has called for the mistress. Shortly, I will face punishment. I have to make this worthwhile.

A groan distracts me from my imminent demise, and I gaze down. The man is so close to death, and I touch his skin. I have only seconds before they will pull me away. Looking deep into his eyes, I stroke his forehead with one hand, and with my other hand, I clasp his.

Hovering over him, I whisper into his ear, "I release you from your pain on earth and send you to Valhalla to serve amongst the bravest of warriors." These are the words that I have heard the winged Valkyries being taught to say as they reap their warrior. I hold his hand and stroke his forehead, but he remains in front of me, still laboring to breathe, his face distorted in pain.

The seconds tick by slowly, and I wonder when he will be sent. The uneventful moments turn into what seem like hours. Deep despair fills me as I watch him remaining in pain, his spirit not leaving, and I feel like I have betrayed him, all the wingless Valkyries, and myself. Not only that, I have also managed to look like a fool in front of the handsome angel of death and my nemesis.

"Oh, get out of the way."

Roughly, I'm nudged aside, and I stumble on top of the soldier. He cries out in pain, making my despair dig deeper, twisting the horrible guilty knife into my heart farther. I couldn't take away his pain as I promised him. It didn't leave.

"You will never be able to reap the warriors," Rota sneers. She kneels beside him and clasps his hand while holding his face, saying exactly the same words I just said to him.

I watch as peace fills his face, his ragged breathing stops, and he lies perfectly still. For him, deep happiness fills me, but at the same time, I want to tear at my enemy. I want to push and shove her. I want to take out all my aggression on her, all my disappointment in myself that I did not prove that the wingless Valkyries are just as valuable as the winged Valkyries. Deep embarrassment sits deep within my soul, causing these urges to be even stronger. I move toward her to play out the actions in my mind when two feet hit the ground right next to me.

My eyes dart up from the form and land on a face with terrifying blue eyes that pierce deep into my soul. Mistress. She is certainly not pleased. Horror whirls in my stomach, and I grit my teeth, knowing what is about to happen.

A hand, gentle but firm, lands on my shoulder, and strange sensations of warmth and cold fill me.

The mistress's eyes dart to my side. "Angel of death, leave."

I turn to realize that it is Harut's hand on my shoulder.

He nods curtly at the mistress once then leans forward and whispers in my ear, "Don't give up. You may find a way." And with that, he pushes off the ground and takes to the sky. He flies with all the grace of a winged Valkyrie in the opposite direction, looking for another warrior that needs to be sent to the underworld.

"You shall return to Asgard now, Valkyrie." The words are spiteful, and it takes all my willpower to face my mistress. "You will be on dragon-stall-cleaning duty for the rest of the month on top of your other cleaning duties."

I groan, and my shoulders slump. As much as I love being around the majestic beasts, it is horrible cleaning up their muck–cleaning out the bones and the rotting flesh and the undigested remnants in their waste. I cast my eyes to the ground. "Yes, Mistress." I see no point in arguing, because I would end up with worse duties.

"How did you even get here, Valkyrie?" Her eyes scrutinize me.

"I snuck past Heimdall when he was distracted by some creature."

"What kind of creature?" It surprises me how everyone is immensely interested in this creature. Either that, or they are trying to find holes in my story.

"I don't know. I've only seen it once before when I stumbled across a dragon's nest, and it was stealing the eggs. It has a hideous look, and it almost seemed like it has some dragon in it because of its wings, yet at the same time, its body is fluffy and misshapen. It struck me that day, and when I saw it today, a deep burning sensation went through the scar that it gave me a couple of years ago when I chased it away from the rare dragon egg."

She raises an eyebrow at me. "You shouldn't have been so foolish as to go into the wild dragon wastelands, anyway. Where is this scar it gave you?"

I pull my sleeve over my shoulder from the neckline and expose the scar that runs from my shoulder and down the top of my arm. She strokes her finger along it.

Her brow furrows as she studies the scar. "There doesn't seem to be anything out of the ordinary with it that would cause it to burn again after such a long time. Are you sure you didn't just imagine it?"

"That would not be possible. The burning was very intense. And it was right here." I indicated the point on the scar. "Like the scar had just been caused again. There is no way that I could have imagined that pain." I am almost insulted by her suggestion.

Her shoulders stiffen, and she tilts her chin upward. "You must tell me if you see this creature again. We cannot have this creature going through Asgard."

After her comment that I might have imagined it, I wasn't in the mood to share any information. But to keep up appearances, I nod. "Yes, mistress." Although deep inside, I can feel the rebellion rising. I would rather learn what this creature is myself than let her find out this information. I will prove our worth as wingless Valkyries.

The rainbow colors of Bifrost open and point down to where we are. I step into its rainbow and am sucked up into the colors before landing flat on my feet in the tower with Heimdall. His scowl is the first thing I see as he regards me with distaste, and I flinch. I am in for it now.

- CHAPTER FIVE -

"Heimdall." Nervousness seeps through my voice. "So nice to see you." I smile broadly, showing off as many teeth as possible.

His scowl deepens, and he steps closer to me, his bulky form towering over me. I am considered average size, and I cannot compare to his bulk. I lean back slightly to look into his eyes, and I try to hold my smile, but it slowly fades from my face.

"How dare you sneak past me, Valkyrie. You have violated many rules of Asgard. You are not allowed to pass these borders without permission or without being accompanied by a winged Valkyrie." He grabs me roughly by the shoulder and turns me toward the bridge, stomping that way. "You are coming with me to visit Odin."

My hands turn clammy, and I lose all feeling in my face. I am definitely in for it now. Though I'd thought cleaning out the dragon stalls for a month was a bad enough punishment, this is worse. My primary goal is to become a reaper and a proud warrior for Asgard and to impress Odin, for myself and the other wingless Valkyries, but my idea is quickly flowing down the sewer.

The walk across Bifrost couldn't go any faster. Each step seems to be a giant leap bringing me closer to the palace gates. We reach the steps and walk up. My heart thumps against my rib cage, wanting to abandon this sinking ship as I am dragged toward the palace. I really don't need this kind of attention from Odin. Heimdall hauls me across the marble floors, past the towering marble walls and sculptures, and pauses in front of the throne. Odin is sitting on his throne, his cloak draping over his shoulders and tumbling down his back. He glares at me with his one eye, the other covered in a patch from the time he traded it for wisdom. In a sick sense, I am glad that he can only stare at me with one eye. It is intimidating enough. No words are needed from Heimdall.

"What do we have here?" Odin's eye narrows on me. It is evident that he knew instantly by the way I am being handled and dragged by the gatekeeper that I have caused mischief.

Heimdall pushes me closer to Odin. I feel exposed with nowhere to hide. "This one has defied the laws and snuck behind my back, leaving Asgard without permission. I do not know why you have created these Valkyries without wings. They are no use to us and cause nothing but trouble."

Odin's glare is so intense that I fold to my knees, only sparing a glance through my eyelashes with my chin tilted. "Forgive me, great Odin. I was merely trying to prove my worth on the battlefield. I hope that I have a higher purpose than cleaning halls and dragon pens."

Odin stands, clasping his staff in one hand, and towers over me when he approaches. "Why? Why do you feel like you need to be more? All places are of high importance. And your place and your kind were brought here to serve the winged Valkyries and the gods–to make their living smoother and give them more time to fulfill their duty."

"Yes, great Odin." I know that I should leave it here, but I can't help myself. "I understand, but I would like to be more than just an ordinary slave." When his scowl deepens, I say quickly, "I think that we would be of great service to you."

"Could you reap any?" he asks while pulling his shoulders back, giving him a mightier appearance.

I drop my gaze to the floor and shake my head. "No. I could not."

"Your kind has not been given the talent to reap the souls for Valhalla."

"But there must be a way that we can serve better. Something else we can do in the field to help."

He tsks then huffs a short laugh. "No. There is not." He turns to Heimdall. "How did she escape?"

The mighty gatekeeper tilts his head downward. "I was distracted by some kind of beast. It came and attacked me at the same time that she approached. It's almost as though they were working together."

When I gasp, Odin casts me a warning look before returning his focus to Heimdall. He rubs his chin between his thumb and index finger. "What kind of beast?"

"I don't know. I've never seen it before. It had dragon-like wings and a furry body. It was hideous. It must be a creation—perhaps some kind of witch or god has been mucking around with the creatures of the world. The timing of her escape was too perfect not to suspect that they were working together."

"Oh no." I start to rise until Odin shoots me a glare, and I stop halfway and slowly return to a kneeling position and bow my head. "I was not working with the creature, mighty Odin. I do not know where it came from. I have only seen it once before when it was stealing dragon eggs."

"Stealing dragon eggs, you say?" The eyebrow over his one eye lifts.

"Yes. The egg of the emperor dragon."

"The rare, vicious breed that nobody can get near?"

I nod and ignore the disbelief in his eyes. "I managed to scare the creature off, and it dropped the egg. It also scratched me at the same time."

Odin held his stomach and gave a deep, rumbling laugh. "A creature of some sort stealing the vicious dragon eggs, the golden ones. That is one game creature. What would it be doing with dragon eggs?"

Heimdall says, "I have seen some dragon eggs being traded on the black market. I believe they are being bought and raised as weapons of war, trained to fight, and the golden dragon would be the leader of the pack, able to control all the other dragons. If a commander were to get their hands on one of those dragons and tame it, then they would be in charge of all the dragon world. This could lead to a massacre."

I look at Heimdall with disbelief. "Do they ride these dragons?"

"Of course they ride them. What else would they use the dragons for?" He looks thoughtful for a moment. "I guess other than their vicious fighting skills where they can demolish any being in no time, including giants, and turn them into a meal." He shrugs.

"Then why don't we use dragons to fight?" I look at Odin. "Couldn't the wingless Valkyries join in and help fight for the good warriors alongside the winged Valkyries by riding the dragons? We have been trained as warriors. It would make sense if we were given the opportunity to ride something with wings to help fight for the time that Ragnarok comes. You will need us as well as the few Valkyries you have to help fight in Ragnarok for Asgard and Midgard. We could become protectors rather than servants." A new sense of worth is flowing through me, and before I realize what I am doing, I have half risen to my feet again.

"Do not stand in my presence, Valkyrie. I have not permitted you." Odin's gaze turns vicious again. "You are being ridiculous. Wingless Valkyries are only good and created for what you are doing now. You are nothing more."

A strong voice rumbles through my head. *Do not listen to him, young Valkyrie. You have much to prove.*

My head shoots up, and my eyes dart everywhere. "What?"

"What's wrong with you, Valkyrie?" Annoyance is written all over Heimdall's face. I am staring at him because he is the only other person in the room.

"Did you just say something?"

"No, I didn't."

Odin stamps his staff on the ground, and a crack echoes through the large room. "Your nonsense has caused enough trouble today, young Valkyrie. You must leave and clean the stalls. I have enough to deal with over the rumors of frost giants entering Asgard without permission."

I look at Odin in shock as he points to the door of the hall. Heimdall grabs me by the shoulder and leads me out again. As I am escorted across Asgard, my eyes dart everywhere as I search for the owner of the voice. *Who could have spoken to me, especially when it appears that the two men didn't hear the voice?*

- CHAPTER SIX -

Argh! The smell is disgusting. The potent odors of regurgitated flesh follow me around as I scoop it up from the floor of a dragon's cave. The solid rock walls have successfully managed to trap the smell within the enclosure. Heimdall commanded me to grab my shield and get changed into my oldest clothes, and pointed to the dragon stall that I had to clean first. Naturally, it was the most potent. Without any extra hands, I sling my shield over my back and shovel up the muck and carry it toward the chasm. The dragon stalls are built within the solid rock of the mountains in chasms or cliff faces.

The current occupant of this particular stall is a blue dragon that despite being smaller than other dragons, still towers above me. When I look at this specific breed, it is hard for me to believe that all dragons are classed as aggressive. The blue dragon has a smaller snout and lacks the horns of the other breeds, and its eyes have an innocent look. Its scales are a medium-blue color edged with white, making its overall color seem lighter than it is.

This young male's blue eyes watch me intensely as I clean out his mess. Despite his look of innocence, I make sure I keep my eye on him. I have been warned to regard all dragons with caution at all times. As I walk toward the edge of the cave to throw the pile of trash over the mountain's side, he runs at me, breathing out a plume of fire.

I dart forward and trip on a rock, dropping the shovel and falling flat on my stomach. My face narrowly misses the pile of manure that I just gathered. Something warm and gooey wraps around my arm, and I realize that my arm was not so lucky. "Yuck!" I shake my hand, trying to rid it of the horrible smelly slop.

A strange sound comes from the dragon. I managed to miss the plume of fire, and remembering it, I suddenly jump to my feet and turn to face the dragon, who has just proven that despite his looks, I must treat him with caution. The winged Valkyries are raising these dragons to be aggressive so that they can be fighting practice. Despite knowing this, I am curious as to why this dragon has had a go at me. Except when I face the dragon and meet his blue eyes, his head is jerking up and down, and his teeth are showing.

I blink a couple of times, trying to clear my vision, because I am having trouble believing what I am seeing. Cocking my head, I ask, "Are you playing with me?"

The dragon pushes his shoulders back and spreads his wings wide, showing off the decorative white dots that resemble stars across the blue membranous wings. He looks much larger than seconds before, and he wipes the smirk off his face and gazes at me with his big eyes. Suddenly, he narrows his eyes and shoots out a long plume of fire. I move aside with my back toward him, narrowly missing the edge of the cliff. When I spin around and look at the dragon again, he is doing the same thing as before, sitting on his butt, making a funny sound, bobbing his head up and down, and showing off his teeth.

I observe the dragon for a moment. "You are playing with me, aren't you?"

He can't come any closer to me because of the chain around his rear leg. I have not cleaned out this particular dragon's stall before. In fact, I haven't had much to do with the blue dragons, so I am surprised when this one stands up and starts to wag his tail.

"Okay. I will play. But can you stop throwing plumes of fire at me? I prefer not to be seared." I stand ready with my legs shoulder width apart, braced for the next move.

The dragon's eyes widen. He seems to realize what I am doing, and his tail wagging increases speed, knocking aside scattered bones behind him. My arm still stinks and feels disgusting, but I'm not about to turn my back, in case he throws another plume of fire at me.

I look for something on the ground that I can throw, so that maybe he will chase it like a dog. As I do this, I see a bright-orange light coming in my direction, and I dodge. I have no time to grab my shield, and I block it instinctively with my arm that is covered in manure.

As I feel the searing pain from the fire, I curse myself for my stupidity, though it isn't a direct hit because I dodged far enough away. Yanking my arm away, I stare at the damage. I am surprised to see that the manure has protected my arm from damage, and all that my arm suffered from was the extreme heat. I expel a breath. "That was close."

Next time, I won't be so stupid. The muck around my arm has dried, and I peel it away. The dragon seems to be laughing again, and his back legs jump up, and his tail starts to wag.

Instantly, I brace myself and throw up a hand while the other reaches for my shield. "Stop. No. Don't do that. You're going to hurt me. I would love to play, but I don't want to be hurt." I feel ridiculous talking to a dragon, but maybe he can understand me. After all, the emperor dragon I ran across a couple of years ago could. I can only hope.

Yet his neck vibrates like he is about to send out another plume of fire. I dart forward, as is often recommended when attacking a larger opponent, and manage to duck under the plume of fire, then I grab him around the neck and swing my leg over him. I fling my arms around his neck and sit up straight with my legs bracing his torso and clasp onto his scales. "There. Now I've got you."

He cocks his head and peers at me with one eye. At first, his eyes widen with surprise, then they seem to do that funny smile again, followed by the noise I have worked out to be a chuckle. Suddenly, my whole body tilts forward as the dragon rolls onto his back. I tumble quickly to the side, land on the ground, and somersault to my feet. The dragon lies on his back with his big eyes staring at me and that chuckle jerking his torso.

"You like that, do you? What about this?" I

dart forward and sit on his belly, trying to tickle his underside. The funny gurgling sound continues, and he rolls from side to side. It must be a lonely life, living in this cave all by himself. He seems to be enjoying any interaction. I can never understand why they keep dragons. They don't need them as fighting opponents. It seems like a waste, having them cooped up like a prize within these caves.

A deep, velvety voice bursts through my head. *You seem to have a way with the dragons.*

I freeze and sit up straight, looking around the cave for the source of the voice.

"Heimdall? Is that you?" I could swear it is the same voice I heard back in Odin's hall. I search everywhere, except as I am doing this, I'm knocked off the dragon as he sits up straight, as though standing to attention, looking toward the entrance.

No. This is not Heimdall. It is a shame to see these dragons cooped up like this, with nothing to live for.

I continue to search everywhere for the source of the voice but find nothing. "Yes. It is a shame. This one seems quite playful. Who are you?"

A deep rumble sounds, and it almost sounds like a chuckle. I don't know what to make of it–if I should be insulted or not.

Let's just say I'm someone who's been watching you for a little while. You treat the dragons with more respect than others. You do not mistreat them like your winged kind. They treat them as though they are nothing, disposable, like beasts to be pushed around and injured–something to practice their fighting skills with. For this, I shall reward you.

I'm confused, my feet rooted in place. I look at the dragon and notice that he has remained at full attention, almost as though saluting a corporal. "I don't understand. Why would I treat dragons any differently than any other animal?"

They are higher than any animal, but you treat them with respect and friendliness.

A strange noise sounds at the cliff entrance of the cave, and I look but can't see anything. My gaze darts to the blue dragon, and it is also looking in the same direction. So I start to search the area again, following the sound, only to see that the massive form of a golden dragon has appeared out of thin air right in front of me. Its eyes are golden and vicious and looking directly at me.

- CHAPTER SEVEN -

It suddenly dawns on me where I have heard
this voice before. This is the mother dragon
that gave me one chance to escape her wrath a
couple of years ago, and I took it. I cannot for
the life of me think why she has sought me out.
As I look into her deep-golden-brown eyes,
they feel as though they are boring into me. I
try to swallow the lump in my throat. The
dragon seems aggressive and intimidating, and
I want to hide. I back up, ready to dart behind
the blue dragon, when I realize that he's also

backing up to hide behind me, and whenever I try to dart around the back of him, he somehow moves quicker. I observe him and wonder what his deal is.

Right as I do this, the golden dragon commands, *Bow!*

I spin around. "Me?"

At the same time, the blue dragon shuffles behind me, and I turn to see him bowing toward the golden dragon. His front legs buckle underneath his weight, his chest touches the ground, and he casts his eyes down. He is in a complete form of submission.

I refocus on the mother dragon. "I-I disappeared as you commanded." My fear rises when I feel her anger. "Why have you pursued me?"

I have been watching you.

"How?"

The emperor dragons have the distinct ability to become invisible, and after you caught my attention, I have been watching you. You have proven to be different from the others. And I have heard your plights to be great.

"Why would you be watching me?"

The dragons have become factious due to this pact with the Valkyries in which we give over one of our clan every year to seal our alliance. It has caused great distrust amongst the dragons, and it is time for the emperor dragon to rule again and unite the dragons. You can only hear my voice because I have allowed you to. Nobody else can hear what I am saying except for the dragon beside you because I have chosen it to be so.

"What do you want of me?"

I am going to lend you this. Beside her, another dragon appears. The dragon is almost identical to her, only smaller. It is young, but its body is at least the size of the blue dragon behind me, and stockier. I stare at the dragon with an open mouth.

"You're going to lend me a dragon? Why?" I can't hide the surprise in my voice.

This is not any dragon. This is my daughter, the egg that you saved from the creature and that you saved from being enslaved in the black market. For as long as you respect her and treat her well, I will lend her to you.

I frown. "Is she a slave to me? Because that is not how I work."

The scowl from the mother dragon's face lifts, and I think it is the closest expression she has to a smile. *No. My daughter and I have discussed this, and she has agreed.*

I look at the smaller dragon, and she nods slightly.

But mark my words—I will be watching you, and she will be reporting back to me. She turns invisible, and I hear the push as she takes off, followed by the flapping of her wings fading away. She has left before I can react.

I call to the empty space, "Thanks."

As I look at the dragon, I'm not quite sure what to do. She studies me with her golden-brown eyes in return. Her horns point menacingly out of the top of her head, and her size is intimidating, even if she is smaller than her mother. Her scales capture the sunlight, and it sparkles off the yellow gold.

Um, hello, Kara. I'm Elan. Her voice is uncertain and sounds much younger than the mother dragon's.

My mouth drops open. I can't believe that they even know my name.

She continues with the uncertainty still in

her voice. *It's nice to meet you. I've heard a lot about you. Please excuse my mother. She is rather a stick-in-the-mud.* She chuckles slightly then stops abruptly. *Oops! Don't let her know that. You know, because I'm supposed to show her respect all the time. After all, she is the leader of the dragons.*

"You're nothing like what I expected." I frown, thinking.

Yeah, no. I'm not like what my mom would expect, either. I do tend to chat a bit—just as a warning. Sometimes I drive my mom crazy. I hope you don't mind. It gets rather lonely out in the fields as a dragon. I see you met my friend Naga. She nods toward the blue dragon. *It was my idea about him playing with you. Sorry about the plumes of fire and all. He doesn't seem to understand that they can hurt you.* She looks at him affectionately. *He's not the brightest of dragons. But I know that he had fun with you.*

I spin around and raise my eyebrow at the blue dragon. He's now sitting up straight and looking eager, not intimidated like when the mother was here.

He's only young, like me. He was the one that

the blue dragons sacrificed this year for the treaty with the Valkyries.

"What is this treaty with the Valkyries?" I ask.

Don't you know? She looks dumbfounded.

I shake my head.

Hmm. That's odd. I would have thought that they would have taught you in Valkyrie school. She cocks her head.

"Sorry, I have no idea."

She folds her legs and lies on her stomach. *The Valkyries and the dragons used to be at war all the time, and the Valkyries made weapons and managed to kill off many dragons, and the dragons used their many gifts to retaliate against the Valkyries. As numbers diminished on both sides, they made an agreement. The dragons would hand over one baby of each clan to the Valkyries as a peace treaty for the Valkyries to stop attacking the dragons. Because of this, the dragons have increased in population. But recently, the dragons have caught on to how the Valkyries are using these sacrificial dragons, and much distrust is building within the dragons and they are becoming factious.*

"Why?"

Because they don't like how the Valkyries are treating their babies, and the dragons selected are not chosen by their own tribes. Another tribe chooses them, with the final decision coming down to my mother. She doesn't say much, but I know it tears her up inside to have to give away the baby dragons. It is also unfair, as we don't have to give up one of the emperor dragons. This is because we are the leaders and our breed is seen as rarer than the other breeds, as we do not have as many eggs. But our breed is known to be more vicious and have more talents. The sacrifice of an emperor dragon is not written in the agreement.

"It seems like a strange sort of agreement. If you don't have to come to live with the Valkyries, why would you want to be lent out to me?"

Oh, I don't want to have to make the decisions of who has to go when I get older and my mom dies. Some of the dragons get quite hurt. Some even die. Being used for target practice with no protection can make them quite aggressive, naturally.

"So why isn't this dragon aggressive? He wanted to play." I indicate Naga, who remains behind me with a vacant look on his face.

That's because he hasn't been put under their tests yet. He's still young and new to the Valkyries. There is still hope that he will remain this way if we can stop them. The other dragons are quite vicious.

"I wouldn't blame them. I would get quite vicious, too, if I kept getting attacked and used only as a weapon and were constantly injured." When I stroke Naga's neck, he nuzzles into my hand, then I turn to look at Elan again, but she has disappeared.

"Where did you go?"

Just then, the stone door slides aside, and in walk Eir and Hildr, my wingless Valkyrie friends from the academy.

"We found you." Eir walks into the cave hesitantly, her eyes on Naga.

After Hildr closes the stone door, she follows, also being wary of the blue dragon. "We've been looking for you forever." Her gaze darts around the room while her fingers twitch over the hilt of her sword. "Who were you talking to?"

I give them a guilty look. "Oh, nobody. I was just muttering to myself as I clean out the pen."

Eir screws up her nose. "It stinks in here. Are you done yet?"

"Almost." I grab the shovel and throw the rest of the mess over the edge of the cliff, then I approach Naga and stroke him briefly on the nose. His eyes widen then dance with excitement.

"That's odd," Hildr says, her hand still twitching over her sword's hilt. "It almost looks like it likes you. I've heard these are dangerous creatures, not friendly ones."

I turn to leave. "I think we're about to find out that that's all wrong. The Valkyries mistreat them. Perhaps they would be different if we treated them with respect."

"Jeez. Did you hit your head while you've been in here? You sound delusional." Hildr grunts as she pulls the stone door open.

I turn around to search the room for Elan, but I still don't see her. I'm about to leave when I hear her in my head.

Meet me at the edge of the cliff above the dragon pens at sundown.

I nod and help Hildr close the door behind us.

- CHAPTER EIGHT -

"Have you been listening to me at all?"
Hildr's runs a hand through her spiky red hair.

I swallow a mouthful of food then cast her a
guilty glance. She only has my attention
because she nudged me in the ribs. My mind is
still focused on the dragons and why they
would pick me. As I look around the dining
hall, I nod. "Sure. You keep going on and on
about how I shouldn't have raced off and gone
to Midgard and how I got myself into trouble.
Blah, blah, blah." I'm pretty sure this is not

what she's been talking about, but I thought I would add it in as a bit of humor.

She rolls her eyes. "It's not all about you, you know."

"I know. I was just adding it in to make it seem like I was listening to something. I'm sure that comment came in somewhere." I shrug and smirk.

"Where is your mind? Have you not been listening at all?" Eir's usually calm face clouds with concern.

I expel a loud sigh. "Listening to what?"

"There have been rumors that the frost giants are trying to invade Asgard and take the throne from Odin," Eir says.

"They will never be able to do that." I scoff. "They have to get past Heimdall." I take a gulp of orange juice.

"Well, *you* did." Hildr fixes her gaze on me. Her freckled face is pale with concern.

I place my glass down. "That was just a fluke. That creature had arrived just in time. It distracted Heimdall, and I have no idea where it came from."

"Maybe the creature works for the frost

giants. Maybe it was testing out how Heimdall can be distracted." Eir flicks her fork against the peas in her cottage pie.

"No. Heimdall will be on high alert now. I've made sure of that. See, not everything I do is bad." I smirk.

Hildr groans and stabs her steak with a knife. "There you go again. Making it all about you."

I gaze around at the other Valkyries in the academy and spot all the winged ones sitting in the best corner. Rota glares at me from the other side of the room.

"You certainly made her a stronger enemy," Eir says before finally shoveling some of her food into her mouth.

"No. If anything, I've embarrassed myself. I couldn't reap the soldier. Though I had the best opportunity ever, I couldn't do it. We're clearly not gifted for that line of work. Still, there must be something we can do to help them in the field."

"Young Valkyrie." The stern voice comes from behind me, and I can't help the shivers that run down my spine.

I spin around. "Mistress Sigrun," I say with the sweetest tone I can muster. "What can I do for you?"

"You haven't finished cleaning the dragon stalls. Hurry up and finish your dinner and go and finish the job. We need these dragons healthy and feisty."

"Yes, Mistress." I have finished my meal, and I am about to get up when I halt. "Mistress, why do we mistreat the dragons?"

If I thought I was in trouble before, that was a mistake. Her voice turns even colder. "The dragons are a vicious breed, and it is in our best interests to learn to fight them to protect ourselves. We do not mistreat them, and it is none of your business as to how we treat them. Your only business is to clean out the stalls." She abruptly turns and walks off.

I sigh then grab my plate and stand, pushing back from the table. "I'll see guys later, okay?"

"Have fun," they say in unison.

"Yep. Because bailing out poop is a whole barrel of fun." Disappointment taints my voice.

~~~~~

I MAKE MY way to the next dragon stall, push back the solid stone door, and enter. This one is in the corner. Its shackle is firmly pressed around its back leg, chaining it closer to the wall, and a muzzle is over its mouth. Its red eyes glare at me, and it puffs out plumes of smoke. This one does not look anywhere near as happy as the last dragon.

I hold up my hands in surrender. "Peace, my friend. I am here to make your living quarters more pleasant. I will not hurt you."

The dragon stomps toward me then stops when its chain runs short. The chain clatters and clangs a few times and quiets when the dragon gives up trying to reach me and slumps in resignation, still glaring at me.

"I'm sorry they treat you this way. I'm going to try to stop them from doing this. I hope you trust me with that."

The dragon says nothing, and a growl rumbles deep within its throat. Keeping my distance, I clean out its water, scoop up its droppings, and throw them over the edge.

This is really not a very nice way for them to live. I do this with a few other dragons and have the same response as I did with the red one. It is breaking my heart to see them like this when I had such a close interaction with Naga and Elan earlier today. They have more to them than being our target practice.

After walking down a stone corridor, I enter another dragon's stall. This one doesn't seem quite so old, but it isn't as playful as Naga. Instead, it cowers in the corner and eyes me suspiciously. It doesn't have a muzzle, but I make sure I stay out of reach, just in case. It has a tremendous ugly sore running down its leg that looks to be made by a sword, and my heart sinks because of how the dragon regards me.

I finish quickly and look out the opening to see the sun setting. Not much light remains in the sky. I promised that I would meet Elan at the top of the cliff, so I have to run, and I scurry out of the dragon's enclosure. Just as I exit the rocks, a high-pitched scream fills the air. Increasing my speed, I search for where this has come from. When I reach a small hill, I climb up it and look around. Another scream fills the air, and my gaze darts in that direction. At a distance not too far away, I can see Rota being thrown around like a rag doll by a frost giant. Other winged Valkyries flock in, ready to attack. As much as I despise them because of how they treat us, I'm not going to let any of them die by a frost giant's hand. They are too crucial to the cause of Valhalla and the future of Asgard with the coming of Ragnarok. I run toward them, unsheathing my sword.

"Wingless, what are you doing here?" Mistress Sigrun glances at me out of the corner of her eye, and I see the annoyance on her face right before she pushes off the ground.

"You have trained us to fight. I am here to help," I call to her as she flaps above me.

"Go and get help instead." She glares down at me. "You cannot fly, and you haven't trained to fight against frost giants."

"No, Mistress. I'm staying to help," I say with determination in my voice while I survey the situation.

Her eyes are like daggers when I chance a look at her. "You have been given an order."

I ignore her final statement, and when I

notice the frost giant is distracted by the Valkyries overhead, I charge toward him and dig my sword into his shin. He bellows in pain, and before I can dart back, his hand swings wide and whips me away from his leg, knocking my sword from my hands and toward the cliff. It clatters several feet away, stopping just on the edge of the cliff, balancing precariously.

Though I long to dart for it, I have second thoughts when the frost giant's large hand swoops down at me again. I dodge the swipe and stand just out of its reach. Something flickers in my peripheral vision, and I look to see Rota's limp form being shaken like a rag doll in front of the different Valkyrie swords. Each time one of the Valkyries attacks the frost giant, they halt only inches away from Rota's body. I have to try something else. Backing away, I search for a hand-sized rock and unclip my sling from the leather strap at the back of my pants. I slide one of several perfect-sized stones I find into the sling and let it fly, aiming at the frost giant's head, and hit him firmly in the temple.

He roars, and I slip another rock into my sling and let it fly before the giant works out where these rocks are coming from. This one hits the giant in the left eye, and he roars louder, holding out Rota's body, almost getting her stabbed by one of her comrades. I step back in shock, trip over a small boulder, and land on my backside. Sharp pain jolts up my torso and down my leg. I glance down to find a place to push off the ground to stand, only to see the giant taking a leap toward me and knocking me firmly off the ground and over the edge of the cliff.

As I fall, I let out a scream and gaze up at the mistress in time to see her eyes widen in horror. While she is distracted, the frost giant swipes at her as though she is a little fly. She too goes flying, except she has her wings to brace her from any fall.

I continue to fall, calling out and wondering what good it will do. I am certain that this is my end. I have achieved nothing, and this will be my fate.

- CHAPTER NINE -

Uh-oh. A voice sounds in my head. *Quick! Turn around!*

"What?"

Flip around so that your stomach faces the ground. Impatience leaks through the voice.

The wind roars in my ears. This is insane. I attempt to flip, and after several tries, somehow, I manage to face the ground instead of falling back first. A golden dragon appears right underneath me just as I slam into her back. I fling my arms around her neck and cling for dear life as Elan glides forward.

Oh, yay! You finally worked it out. It was cutting it fine, though. The ground is only a few feet below.

I peer over her shoulder right as she tilts her wings, narrowly missing a pile of boulders protruding from the ground. When I realize I had only a few more feet to fall before I would have hit the ground, I feel like I want to pass out on her back. She must feel the shift in my mood, because she gazes over her shoulder at me.

"Thank you." After a few seconds of resting on her back, the memory of why I was falling suddenly hits me. "We have to go back and help them," I say with urgency.

You want to save the Valkyries that always belittle you? She gives me a strange look.

I nod.

You're mad. But here we go. Suddenly, she veers in a different direction. I grip her neck tighter, clinging to her scales and feeling their sharp edges digging into my skin. Something gleams in the afternoon sun. It is my sword, which has fallen part of the way down the cliff and is resting precariously on the edge of a rock protruding from the cliff.

I point at it. "I have to grab that first."

She looks at where I'm pointing and maneuvers directly at it. *Get ready!*

"For what?"

For this. Despite me holding on to the scales around her neck, she flicks her body, knocking me off her back and making me free-fall. Panic grips me right down to my core.

"*What are you doing?*" I scream through gritted teeth.

Before she answers, Elan flips around and catches me in her claws. *I can't get you close to the cliff face with my wings. I have to hold you out and hover while you grab the sword.* She flaps her wings until I line up with the surface of the boulder sticking out of the cliff face.

Hop on. She pushes me forward. I land on the rock, pick up my sword, and slide it into its sheath. She spins around the other way, facing out, and looks over her shoulder at me. *Now jump and grab on.*

Too scared to breathe, I brace myself and back up a few steps then sprint and jump off the edge of the boulder, aiming for her head and intending to grasp on to her large horns, but they are just out of my reach, and I start to fall. I reach out, barely managing to wrap my arms around her neck. My body weight pulls me down, and I clasp my hands in front of her throat as I feel myself slip. When I jolt to a halt, I gasp then breathe a sigh of relief when I realize that I am secure. Elan straightens and flies ahead, taking me away from the side of the cliff face. At the same time, she disappears.

"What are you doing? I can't see you."

No. And neither can the frost giant.

"But it will still see me."

You are much smaller than I am, and you will have more of an element of surprise. My body rises and falls as she labors to lift us higher up the cliff face.

We rise high enough to hover above the frost giant and the Valkyries still trying to attack it. I watch as they work in vain. He is much larger than they are, even the tall Valkyries. They are managing to injure him, but with each injury, he is becoming more aggravated and lashing out more. Each time a

Valkyrie flies toward him, he continues to hold out Rota's limp body, blocking the attack. They will not cut one of their own.

Grab your sword. Elan pulls my focus back.

"I hope you know what you're doing," I say as I reach with my right hand and pull the sword from its sheath. The sound of metal grinding against metal is blown away by the wind in the opposite direction of the frost giant.

I'm staying downwind so the frost giant can't smell me, either. Their noses are quite sensitive.

"Okay. I didn't know that. What's the plan?"

I'm going to remain invisible and aim for his neck, and you aim with your sword straight down into his heart.

"Sounds vicious. I like it."

She circles to the front of the frost giant, and if he looks my way, he will see me gliding alone in the air, no wings or anything. It will be strange. The Valkyries, on the other hand, are too busy fighting him off to turn around to see me. Elan flies directly toward him and dodges by a few inches when he flicks his arms to fight off another Valkyrie blocking the view to his neck.

Hook your legs around my neck, and hang on to my scales with your spare arm.

I take her advice, and she flips upside down, dodging his arm. I hold my sword firmly in my right hand.

Moments before we hit, his eyes focus on me, and they widen in surprise. By then, it is too late. He can't even see the dragon and is looking right through her.

As her teeth clamp around his neck, I thrust the sword deep into his heart. I may be upside down and hanging on for dear life, but I still manage to pierce his skin. His knees buckle, and his hand clasps my sword hilt, which is protruding from his chest. He drops the unconscious Valkyrie, and her comrades fly in and catch her up before she hits the ground. They all look confused as to what was happening and are only reacting to the motions of the giant.

The mistress's gaze darts everywhere as she tries to work out what has happened and why the frost giant has fallen. Eventually, she spins around and spots me flying alone in the air with no wings, and watches with wide eyes as I land not far from the ring of Valkyries. Confusion is written all over her face.

Elan giggles. *Look at her face, would you? She still looks annoyed, even though she has no idea what is going on.*

"Young Valkyrie, what are you up to? What have you done? And how on earth are you flying? You don't have wings."

As I feel the thump of the ground underneath Elan, a smile spreads across my face. I watch the gold fill out underneath me as Elan exposes herself. The Valkyries immediately pull back and ready themselves for a fight, their swords aimed directly at my dragon.

"Put your swords down," I say. "She's a friend. She is the reason why the frost giant has fallen. Can you not see the big bite mark around his neck?"

They look too scared to take their eyes off the dragon, but one of the Valkyries quickly looks at the frost giant and sees the large puddle of blood staining the soil beneath him, then she looks at the hilt of my sword, which can just be seen protruding from the frost giant's chest. She regards me with a look of confusion and hesitation before returning to the other Valkyries surrounding Elan.

Apprehensively, the mistress steps toward the dragon and me. Her sword is still half raised, not far from being ready to defend. She looks at me, then back down at Elan, then back up at me.

Elan sits back on her haunches, and I slip down her back and climb off. Then I approach the mistress.

"And why are you sitting on the most dangerous dragon in all of Asgard?" She lowers her sword as I approach.

"This is my friend. She has chosen to be friends with me because I saved her from the creature I told you about when she was an egg. The creature that distracted Heimdall and allowed me to escape past him to Midgard."

"Why didn't you tell me about this? This is a dangerous dragon to have in our area," the mistress barks.

"Yes, she's dangerous. She killed the frost

giant and protected you." I don't hold back my spite, even if she is my mistress. "You should treat her with more respect."

"The only respect to treat dragons with is with distrust. They are dangerous. You will end up getting yourself killed."

I back up and place my hand on Elan's broad golden-yellow snout. She leans into it and brushes herself against my hand like she is used to being petted.

"Yeah. She's extremely dangerous," I say sarcastically. "I'm keeping her with me, and you're not going anywhere near her unless you treat her with respect. If you mistreat her, look out. Not that I need to warn you." I glance over my shoulder. "I'm sure she is more than capable of fending you off better than any dragon you have captured in your caves."

With that, Elan snarls at the mistress, and my instructor backs away.

"Then you must keep her locked away in the cave," the mistress commands. "She must be chained."

"No. She will not be chained. She will sleep where she sees fit, and she will remain free. She came to me of her own free will. I am not going to bind her."

The mistress of Valkyrie Academy eyes Rota, who is still lying unconscious. "We will finish this later, Valkyrie. We must get her to a healer."

- CHAPTER TEN -

The darkness of the night has overtaken the sky, broken only by the beauty of the full moon. After saying goodbye to Elan, I wash off the frost giant's blood in the bathroom and trek toward my dormitory. I am elated over becoming friends with the dragon and managing to take down a frost giant with the help of the dragon. At the same time, my spirits have been knocked down–the mistress still doesn't see me as a warrior and one that could help in the battles. She treats me like a child, and I am not a child. I am almost a grown woman that has been trained in combat. When I reach my room, I kick off my boots beside my bed and flop face-first onto the soft mattress and bury my head in my pillow for a moment.

A shuffling sounds at the door. "Oh Vanir! There you are. I've been so worried about you." Eir rushes to my bedside.

"We've been looking everywhere for you." Hildr stomps in after her. "Where have you been? There has been so much turmoil around. A frost giant has been just outside the academy. It's attacked the winged Valkyries."

I groan, roll onto my side, and prop my head up with my hand as I look at them. "And what would you say if I told you I was there to fight the frost giant?" I study each of them in turn.

Eir clasps her hands and does a little jig. "Were you really?"

Hildr looks at her and shakes her head then nudges her with her elbow. "Of course she wasn't. She can't fly. What's she going to do? Run around and take him out at the knees?"

She rolls her eyes.

"Actually, I took him out with a sword straight into his chest. And the dragon that I was riding tore open his throat."

Hildr makes a guttural noise in her throat in a held-back laugh, but her eyes don't leave my face. I nod and smirk while her mouth drops open and eyes widen.

"You what?" Hildr sits on the edge of my bed, looking as though she is about to fall off.

This time, Eir nudges Hildr firmly in the ribs with her elbow. "See? I told you. She said she would, and she did. And you doubted me!" She poked Hildr in the arm to emphasize the point.

I nod as Hildr continues to stare at me open-mouthed.

"So what did the mistress say?" Eir raises Hildr's jaw with her hand, closing her mouth. "She must be bowing down at your feet, asking you to join them."

"Nope," I say, shaking my head. I push myself up into a sitting position and rest my head in my hands with my elbows on my knees. "She still wants to give me another talking-to."

"What?" Hildr squeaks. "She should be begging you to join them. And what about this dragon? Did you free one and go and ride it?"

"No. It was the strangest thing. This dragon decided to be my friend because I saved her when she was an egg."

"You mean the one you've been bragging about for the last couple of years?" Eir asks.

I nod.

"I thought that was just a story," Hildr says.

"Well, that just shows how much faith you have in me. Do you think I have just been wasting my breath, telling you fibs about my adventures?" I shake my head at her and smirk. I don't blame her. It did seem like a pretty tall tale.

"But wait—wasn't that dragon an emperor dragon?" Hildr asks.

"Yes."

Her jaw slackens.

"Won't they eat you for breakfast?" Eir asks.

"They could. But they promise not to eat me."

"That's a plus. So what now?" Eir secures a

lock of her hair behind her ear.

I shrug. "I don't know. The mistress is still determined to keep me in the bad corner. I would have thought my defeating the frost giant with the help of the dragon would have boosted her confidence in me. I hoped that it would show that we are more than just scrubbers and cleaners, more than ones to pick up after the winged Valkyries, but she seems stuck in that mindset. I am still planning on changing this."

Kara! Elan's voice calls clearly.

"What is it?" I ask, and I stare at the wall as I concentrate on her voice.

It looks like you have a problem.

"What do you mean?"

"Who are you talking to?" Hildr's voice breaks through my thoughts.

My eyes focus on the room, and I remember that Hildr and Eir are with me. "Oh, don't worry. I'm not going mad. I'm just talking to Elan, my dragon."

"It talks to you?" Eir asks.

"She," I correct her. "And yes."

"Where is she?" Hildr searches everywhere

in the room, and tension stiffens her body.

"Not in here. Shh. She is trying to tell me something important." I hold my index finger up to my lips. "What's the problem, Elan?"

Odin is coming your way, and boy, he looks cranky.

My shoulders slump, and my dormitory door flies open. The mistress and Odin block the entrance. My eyes land on Odin. Elan was not exaggerating.

The End

ACKNOWLEDGMENTS

I am touched by the enormous amount of support I have received from my immediate family. My husband has been a helpful first reader and at times been a wonderful motivator, with hints of ideas to help me through the blanks. The support from my three sons has also been overwhelming. They have put up with my head being in the clouds, thinking about the next plot twist or story for several years. Along with many hours spent working on my books and keeping in touch with my readers.

A big thank you to my extended family who support me being a book enthusiast.

A huge thank you to my editor, Susannah Driver, her editing and writing tips, and my Proofreader, Kristina B, for picking up the things we missed.

Thank you to all of my readers who have loved my work, and continue to read my stories.

Book 2 of Valkyrie Academy Dragon Alliance Series 'Vanished' released August 2019.

BOOKS BY KATRINA COPE

~~~~~

Pre-Teen Books

THE SANCTUM SERIES

JAYDEN'S CYBERMOUNTAIN

SCARLET'S ESCAPE

TAYLOR'S PLIGHT

ERIC & THE BLACK AXES

ADRIANNA'S SURGE

~~~~~

Young Adult Urban Fantasy

AFTERLIFE SERIES

FLEDGLING

THE TAKING

ANGELIC RETRIBUTION

DIVIDED PATHS

Afterlife Novelette

THE GATEKEEPER

~~~~~

Young Adult Urban Paranormal Fantasy

SUPERNATURAL EVOLVEMENT SERIES

(Associated with the Afterlife Series)

WITCH'S LEGACY (#0.5 Prequel)

AALIYAH

~~~~~

Young Adult Fantasy Nordic Myths

VALKYRIE ACADEMY DRAGON ALLIANCE

SERIES

MARKED (Prequel)

CHOSEN

VANISHED

SCORNED

INFLICTED

EMPOWERED

AMBUSHED

GET UPDATES & NOTIFICATIONS OF GIVEAWAYS

Would you like a FREE copy of Marked?
Visit here:
https://www.katrinacopebooks.com/valkyrie-academy-dragon-alliance
Through this link you can sign up for my newsletter and receive a FREE copy of Marked plus updates about my fantasy books, sales and notification of giveaways.

DID YOU ENJOY THIS BOOK?
YOU CAN MAKE A BIG DIFFERENCE.

Honest reviews of my books help bring them to the attention of other readers.

If you've enjoyed this book, I'd be grateful if you could spend a few minutes leaving a review (it can be as short as you like).
The review can be left on Amazon and Goodreads.
Thank you very much.

ABOUT THE AUTHOR

Katrina is an author of several Young Adult and Preteen/Middle Grade novels. Each of her released books reaching the top 100 in certain categories on the Amazon's Best Sellers Rank – a few even as high as number one.

She resides in Queensland, Australia. Her three teenage boys and husband for over nineteen years treat her like a princess. Unfortunately though, this princess still has to do domestic chores.

From a very young age, she has been a very creative person and has spent many years travelling the world and observing many different personalities and cultures. Her favourite personalities have been the strange ones, yet the ones under the radar also hold a place in her heart.

During her last extensive travels, she spent 16 nights in a bomb shelter on a Kibbutz 8 kilometers off the Lebanese border. It was to avoid Katyusha bombs that the resident volunteers decided to name her after (she is still trying to work out why).

Katrina's online home is at www.katrinacopebooks.com
You can connect with Katrina on:
Twitter https://twitter.com/Katrina_R_Cope
Facebook https://www.facebook.com/Author.Katrina.Cope

Instagram
https://www.instagram.com/katrina_cope_author
Pinterest
https://www.pinterest.com.au/katrinacope56
Email authorkatrinacope@gmail.com

Made in the USA
Columbia, SC
13 January 2021